Mr Bear & the Bear

D0318357

Frances Thomas is donating 50% of her royalties for *Mr Bear & the Bear* to Libearty, the world campaign for bears. The Libearty campaign was launched in 1992 by the World Society for the Protection of Animals to raise international awareness of the threats facing all species of bear. One of their most successful projects has been the building of two sanctuaries for the rescue and rehabilitation of 'dancing' bears, saving them from a life of misery and abuse.
For more information write to:
WSPA, Libearty Campaign,
Freepost, London N4 1BR

A Red Fox Book

Published by Random House Children's Books
20 Vauxhall Bridge Road, London SW1V 2SA

A division of The Random House Group Ltd
London Melbourne Sydney Auckland
Johannesburg and agencies throughout the world

Text Copyright © Frances Thomas 1994
Illustrations Copyright © Ruth Brown 1994

3 5 7 9 10 8 6 4

First published in Great Britain by
Andersen Press Ltd, 1994
Red Fox edition 1997

This book is sold subject to the condition that it shall not, by way of trade or otherwise, be lent, resold, hired out, or otherwise circulated without the publisher's prior consent in any form of binding or cover other than that in which it is published and without a similar condition including this condition being imposed on the subsequent purchaser.

The right of Frances Thomas and Ruth Brown to be
identified as the author and illustrator of this work
has been asserted by them in accordance with the
Copyright, Designs and Patents Act, 1988.

Printed in Singapore by Tien Wah Press (PTE) Ltd

THE RANDOM HOUSE GROUP Limited Reg. No. 954009

www.randomhouse.co.uk

ISBN 0 09 972611 4

Mr Bear & the Bear

Story by Frances Thomas
Pictures by Ruth Brown

Everyone called him Mr Bear, though perhaps he had another name. "Cross as a bear," people said. Nobody smiled at him in the street, children stuck their tongues out behind his back. Dogs growled and cats ran away.

He had lived for many years in the big house on the hill.
Behind was a large garden with trees and a high wall all
around. Mr Bear grew older and crosser in the dark house.

One day he had to go to town to get his spectacles
mended. The town was noisy and full of people.
The crowds pushed him this way and that, and he found
himself in the town square with roundabouts and jugglers
and stalls selling gingerbread and sugar plums.

A man held a stick and chain. On the other end of the chain was a bear, with a ring through his nose. His mouth was kept shut by a muzzle. There were shackles on his back paws. He was smelly and his coat was matted as an old rug. His eyes were dull and runny.

When the man poked him, the bear had to stand on his hind legs. The man poked again, and the bear jumped, lumbering from one foot to another. It looked as if he were dancing and all the people laughed and clapped their hands.

But Mr Bear could see that the bear did not dance for joy.
"Dance!" said the man. The bear danced and the
people clapped.

Mr Bear left the square and the town and went slowly up the hill to the dark house. He looked cross as he walked. "Cross as a bear," people said.

That night he could not sleep. He did not remember the music or the roundabouts, but he thought of the bear with the sad dull eyes.

Then he sat up in bed. He looked crosser than ever. But he had an idea.

Very early the next morning, he got his horse and wagon and set off for town. Almost no-one was about, except the street sweeper and the baker opening his shutters and yawning. But all the wagons and roundabouts had gone, all the striped tents and gingerbread stalls.

Mr Bear saw a small girl carrying water.

"Where did the fair go?" he asked.

"That way," she said, pointing.

Mr Bear did not thank her. The little girl shook her head. "Cross as a bear," she thought.

Mr Bear left the town. The sun rose in
the sky, and the road was wide and dusty.
    At midday he saw the man by the side of
the road, eating a sausage. His horse was
eating grass. And there in a cage, eating
nothing at all, slumped the dirty old bear.

"I've come to buy your bear,"
said Mr Bear to the man.
    The man laughed and took another bite
of sausage. Mr Bear took out his purse, and
showed the man a gold piece.
    "The bear isn't for sale," said the man. Mr Bear
showed him another gold piece. And another.
The man yawned.
    "I've had enough of bears anyway. Too cross.
Take him. I'll stick to juggling in future."

They lifted the cage on to the wagon. The bear growled. Mr Bear took apples from his bag and fed them to the bear. The journey home was long and bumpy. When the bear growled, Mr Bear gave him more apples. In that way they got home, though by the time they did, it was nearly dark.

That night, in Mr Bear's woods, the bear slept well. Mr
Bear had given him a strong sleeping potion. While he
slept, Mr Bear took off the chain and muzzle. He broke the
shackles. He chopped up the cage and burned it.

   While the bear slept, he dreamed. He dreamed of the
time long ago, when he had played in the hills with his
mother, his brothers and sisters. He remembered splashing
in the silvery water and catching fish. He remembered
rolling in soft grass, and sniffing for ripe berries.

   Then he dreamed of the time the hunters came. They
took the bear and his brothers and sisters and sold them.

When he remembered this, it made him wake with an angry growl. Then he opened his mouth wide and yawned. He lifted up his head and stretched. There was no chain to jerk him back to the ground; no cold slippery cage, only soft, sweet grass. He stood up unsteadily, on his four paws. He could smell delicious water.

He took one step, then another. Still no chain stopped him. Nobody shouted at him or hit him. Into the stream he lumbered, and splashed, slowly at first, then faster. Cool water ran down his dry matted fur, his burning throat and into his sticky jammed-up eyes.

When he shook himself all over, he remembered how
hungry he was. Across the garden, sitting quietly on the
grass, was the man who had given him apples.
He liked apples.

And there was more: porridge, honeycomb and nuts.
The bear ate everything up. He had not eaten
such delicious things for a long time. He looked
at Mr Bear, who looked back at him. Mr Bear smiled.